THE MYSTERIOUS BRIDGE

JEEVANANDHAM.G

Made with ♥ on the Notion Press Platform
www.notionpress.com

Contents

Preface

This book was wriiten by jeevanandham who is a student, he was born on May 13 ,2001, he completed his secondary in 2019 and collegein 2022, this is the second book of the author, the first book of the author is The Journey of Love, which was published in the year 2021, and in this book it was divided into two parts the first par is "The Mysterious bridge" and the second part of the book which talk about the continuation of the firsr book the author who writes his book in the fictional manner, The Mysterious Bridge which talks about the bridge, which has the incidents occurs in a fishy manner, The Journey of Love Chapter II which speaks about the management of the the married life.

CHAPTER ONE

THE MYSTERIOUS BRIDGE

Introduction:

This story is written by Jeevanadham who was born in Pondicherry, India, in May 2001, he completed his secondary in 2019 in Pondicherry, and his Undergraduate in Tagore arts and science college, Pondicherry in 2022, the first script is "The Journey of Love", which is a story of a couple from a different nation was published in 2021. And the author of the story is from India (Pondicherry), this is a fictional story with a social message, this book which contains about two stories, the first part of the book, which speaks about the mysterious incidents occurs in the village bridge, and the second part of the book contains the second chapter of “The Journey of lovc”

The Hero’s name is Dhruv, he is a member in Microsoft headquarters in the United States of America (U.S), earns $62,571 per month, he married a white, by convincing his Parents, Dhruv is a brown skin, he leads a smooth life with his wife Charlotte and 3 children. Atfirst, they met in a cafeteria, and he falls at first sight, Dhruv is a kind person, who donates his food or clothes to the poor people and he is in the leadership of protestors for black liberty, which inspires charlotte to be a life partner of Dhruv. And they make a meeting at a certain time, after sometimes, Charlotte invited Dhruv to her home, and she introduced Dhruv to her parents, at first they hesitate to accept, but after sometimes they get to accept the marriage, then they get married at a church in a grand manner, another side the issue was unknown to Dhruv's parents, after sometimes he makes a call that I get married with a White skin, which is a storm to Dhruv's parents because they get seeing a pride to him, finally, they get convinced after 5 years, then now its 2028 January 4, He had a call from his parents that Dhruv younger sister has a pride, Dhruv with a smile said that "I feel delighted to hear the news" and he ensures that he will carry over the marriage, his Parents feel happy and enquires about his life and Charlotte for some times and they ends the call, he passed on the information to charlotte, she felt happy, then they reserves the tickets, after some days they arrived to India on 12.02.2028, his family waited to catch Dhruv at the airport. Dhruv arrives on a noon flight, with his wife, when they arrive in India, the relatives and his parents feel happy to meet, and they lunch with the couple, then while traveling, Dhruv and charlotte enjoy nature, Dhruv enquires about the village and people, They travel over a bridge called "Cauvery Bridge" at Vellore which connects to their village, Dhruv's father says about the mysterious bridge that "he heard about mysterious deaths on the bridge", then they reached their home by evening 7:00, charlotte arrives to India for the first time, the family gave them a warm welcome to the couple, the atmosphere is pretty with a smile, Dhruv balances the event. Dhruv's father is a kind and well-known man in the village and so Arjun das, a well-known politician is invited to the marriage, he arrives day before the marriage, visits the village people's farm lands, he asks about the issues of the village, then that night he attends the reception, he stays in a hotel that night, while he is sleeping, he heard someone mourning, suddenly he wakes, he washes his face, while he washing his face, the water turns to reddish and he contacts the receptionist, he tells about the issue and he gets slept again. The next day he attends the marriage, he spends the day with the villagers and he gets off from the village at night, while he drives near the bridge the area surrounds with a strong breeze and it starts raining, while he drives on the bridge the road gets cracked and broken, the car fall under the bridge and struck on the tree while he tries to be out that moment, he saw an unnatural thing, which hangs him in the branch of the tree. The next day the spot undertook by the escort, experts and the vehicle is taken from the river, the body looks so horrible, and the department investigates the surroundings, but there are no clues or suspects there, the blood samples are collected by the experts, after sometimes, Dhruv found a piece of ribbon and he gave the ribbon to forensic experts department, the family requested to Dhruv and Charlotte that leave to oUnited States, but Dhruv refused to leave the town and his wife withstand with his decixion, they start the investigation about the death, that how the minister had killed suspiciously, most people gave their response, as it is an old bridge or he may be drunk and drive at that night, when Dhruv sat under a tree an old person with stick arrived to him, he asked about Dhruv and he introduces himself, he investigates about the bridge issue, which is fishy, the old man gets so nervous and reluctance to speak about the issue. After some time the old man started about the issue. It was a girl who was killed by the minister, Dhruv can't understand his words and he continue explaining that her name was Hema, who is smart with her activities and hyper too, but her fate for her is wrong, she was born into a family who is not accepted by the village, because of the wealthy peoples in the village, they make several burdens, but Hema's family not care about it so, they made a master plan, all these because they are not wealthy, so the wealthy people, separate the family to out of the village and the distance between them and wealthy ones is a paddy field and it too surrounded by a copper fence. There are two non-wealthy families, who get partnered with each other, they share everything, lived happily. One day Hema's friend Priya, tried to enter the village, so she asks Hema to help her, at first Hema refused, but after, she accepts with it, so they had a toolkit, they cut the part of the copper fence and they enter into the paddy land, they played for some time and they return to their home, when their parents questioned about their absence, they reply with silly reasons like, we get hangout, and they continue the thing. One day I saw Priya and Hema playing in the paddy field, and I asked them to get off the field, I saw the wire had been tanned and after some time, I dump the copper fence for that time, a man enters the field, who notices me and questioned that what happened over here? I reply that the wire gets rusted so I am replacing the wire and he gets slight doubt my response, he silently left the place, the man make the news like the flu, and they make the two families, appear before the Panchayat committee, the news gets to Hema and Priya's parents, they stood before the Panchayat committee and they argue with the issue, the Panchayat as for the solution to the public, the 50% of the villagers said to hang-up, some said to give warning, 20% percent said to give less punishment after sometimes they decided to give less punishment that is to stand on the field for 2 days without food, they appointed a person to supervise, whether they are following the rule, after two days the Panchayat was formed again and get into a final decision they said that one family should vacate the village and enter into the city, then the panchayat gets dismissed, that night Hema's family gets away from the village side, Priya felt heartbroken and sad. After some days they arrived in Madras city, Hema can't forget the memories of the village, and Priya and her parents joined her in a Public school, in a short span she combined with new friends, but she has deep remembrance of Priya. One day she met a friend who has a close enough attitude to Priya, her name is Abirami and she sat next to Hema, they get introduced to each other, they gather for everything and Hema always remember Priya, one day Hema make a call to Priya and spoke for hours and Hema shared about her life, she asked about Priya's family and the villagers, she replied its perpetual which makes Hema, so disturbed, she hang-up the call. Hema decided to be an IAS officer, so she makes her studies smart and wilful. Hema score high in both in SSLC And HSLC, which is a nice slap for the villagers and she joined in the integrated course in Pondicherry University for an degree in Political science , on other side, she prepare for the UPSC exam, which makes her career better, she clears her exams in the attempt, she became an graduate, but Unfortunately it is not applicable for UPSC, she didn't lose her hope and tried her best, When she completed her course in year 2000 with an Post-graduate state, she enter into an other side of life that is she gets selected in an IAS interview, Priya get so glad of the information, then Priya get an inspiration from her friend and she get off from the village for higher studies which makes panic for the villagers, Priya went to Coimbatore with her mother to pursue her higher studies, at first they lived in an rent house by doing housemaid works, Priya gets better in her studies participated in sports competition and she won medals, prizes with an scholarship, she informed to Hema, which makes Hema proud of her friend, this was heard by the villagers, which makes them so jealous, that how can a low categorized girls can get those appreciation and skill, and the wealthy people makes a plan on other side, Hema joined on duty in Vellore district, which get flashed in the news. The old man ends with the information, and he get off from the place, then Dhruv have some information about Hema, then he went to the house, but he found some suspicious things around him, then he reached the home and he gets interacts with his family, then he asks his parents that can I stay here for some days, the parents and they gets accepted with Dhruv's request, then he gets to bed, in his inner mind he feels something strange, then he washes his face he notices that the face Mirror gets smashed, when he calls his parents the glass turns to normal form, Dhruv's parents enquires about him, then he turns to bed, the next day he went out with his wife, on the way he met several obstacles, the climate turns cloudy, he crossover a house which is under mystery, while he drives on the bridge he saw someone walking on the mid of bridge, when he horns and move forward the figure gets vanished, and his wife question that why you do horn on the bridge, which Is fishy to him, they went to a restaurant they had lunch, then he enquires with the manager about Hema, the manager's father get interrupted with his Dhruv's conversation, that I saw her as you said, that she worked as an employee without the knowledge of her mother. After some time, I heard that she became an IAS of Vellore district, in the year 2000, then they went to a temple of Kanchipuram, and while returning to their home, Dhruv's noticed that the bridge road filled with blood, and the tire gets struck into a dig, while he tries to move the vehicle, he was helped by women and he does thank her, his wife question that to whom do you thank? which gets into an doubt to Dhruv, he saw again an ribbon on the bridge, then they arrive to their home, after he gets relaxed the family get enquires about the day, with smile he explained the day was fine, he gets a dream that Hema gets a betray with someone, the next day he was hearing the news that" the ex-minister who give approval for bridge with unapproved cements" gets assassinated the manner of killing is just equivalent to the Dhruv's dream, which gets so fishy to Dhruv, then he went to the spot, he look for the evidence, he saw a date which is written in blood "03.06.2003" and it makes sense to Dhruv, then he visits his friend, who is a forensic expert he return to his home and he heard that his wife had exit before an hour and not yet returned home, Dhruv make a call to her, where she can't attend his call, which makes Dhruv doubtful, then he waits for her arrival, she arrived by 03:00, then he questioned that "where have you went", she replied that I have went for a ride in the car, to the town, then Dhruv leave about the issue, the next day he heard the news that the contractor of the bridge gets assassinated in a mysterious way which is a undefined answer to Dhruv, then he went to the nearby library and he search for the article on the date 03.06.2003, then at first he can't find the article and then he found the article then, he gain the knowledge, about it, then he return to home, and he speak to his parents about the issue, again he notice that his wife coming at late night which makes him more doubtful, then he follow her, his attitudes were abnormal, and he plan to take for a dinner, when he notices that she is using her right hand usually, Charlotte is a left handed person and he asks to his wife that "why are you using your right hand for dinning? " she replied that I'm practicing with the Indian tradition which strikes to Dhruv, then when returning to the home, she asks for some books which is related to administration, Dhruv accept with the request, and they return to home, and they went for sleep in the same night he had a dream which is in the horrible manner, suddenly he woke and thinks for some time, he saw that his wife gets roaming in the floor, and he calls by her name, but there is no response from her, and he went nearby her, a hand touches him, and his wife questioned what happened and they went for sleep, the next day he heard the news that the home minister is arriving to Chennai to inaugurate the idol of peace, then he notices some herbal ingredients for beauty, and he question to his mother that did you made this ingredients, then her mother replied that, absolutely, your partner pretends for this, then he went for a bath, he saw a date which is written in blood, in the mirror 22.09.2028, which is the upcoming day, so he gets doubt, after his bath, he searches his wife but he hears a singing voice in the upstairs, he stick to the karaoke, when he close to the karaoke gets halt, then he knocks the door, but charlotte came from the pavement, and questioned Dhruv, then they went downstairs, she asked Dhruv lets drive for Chennai, and he accepts with her request, and he kept an eye with Charlotte, the next day, they went to Chennai, firstly they went to the restaurant and they have their breakfast, while having breakfast they saw the headlines as the home minister arrived to Chennai airport , at the peak and tourist places are under block or with Z squad, protection, so, he make a request with charlotte that we return to home, for that she reply with positive response, when exit Chennai, the home minister vehicle went on the bridge and the bridge gets renovated recently, it gets cracks and vehicle went under the bridge which is a water boundaries, that time the Home minister saw a horrible outlook of Hema, and he screams that " aww... please leave me, and I'm not responsible for it" and the vehicle drowns into the water and the cameras and media get crashes, after an hour the vehicle get out of the water, but the minister gets vanished from the vehicle and the traffic gets cleared, then, Dhruv look at charlotte who hang up with sleep, then they went to the village, after arriving they get fresh up, Dhruv who make a confidential talk with his parents that the activities of charlotte gets suspicious and they went for sleep the next day, they call for a psychologist, and it is a great surprise for Hema, because she is Abhi, who is her schoolmate, then Abhi gets identify its Hema, with her activities and she got onto the mental check-up, after end of the process, Abhi intimate that she is affected with some issues for the moment I suggest some medicines and take care of her, she left the house with smiling at Hema, then on the end of the day charlotte intake the medicines, the night again, Dhruv gets the mourning voice, he follows the voice and he stick to the voice and he ascend the stairs, and he feels like someone gets backing him, charlotte is standing behind him but the murmuring voice from the other side of the door, and he break the door, he saw and get astonished with the incident because, he saw that, charlotte drowse in the bed, and he saw that his mirroring behind and he yell at the mirror face and suddenly step down into his chamber and lock the door, the next day he elaborate to his family about the issue and they glance him for a moment and they cackle at him, which, makes

Dhruv upset, he plan to make for an evidence, so he attach the surveillance cameras in his chamber, then he ask his parents that "shall we hangout for a while", they insisted charlotte to accompany with them but, she refused. Then, they went to the nearby spot and Dhruv asked to watch the live video, and he vanished, after a while, they were keen on it, they noticed something fishy over it, they noticed the abnormal attitudes of charlotte, they make an eye on it, then they went to the temple and make a wish to the God, then they returned at night, then they went to the bed the parents discussed the issue with themselves , then they slept, the next day, the psychologist gave a revisit to the house, he met Dhruv to give a piece of information about charlotte, when Abhi met with Dhruv, she said that "the reports of charlotte are suspicious," Abhi questioned Dhruv that "whether you notice anything changes in her?" Dhruv responded yes of course doctor. Firstly, she is using turmeric for baths, usually, she uses soap or other cosmetics, Secondly I found something!!! See over here, usually, she hates chocolates, but nowadays she like chocolates of the specified brand which makes sense, here are some chocolate covers, and I found something from the trashcan, here is a pamphlet with the marking of date in the pamphlet, then Abhi takeover the chocolate paper, and she requested that "can I take a look in Charlotte room? Dhruv responded Of course, Abhi found a secret lock in the room, then they unlock it with a hammer, inside the locker they found some chocolate covers, mystery codes, some hazardous weapons, a book, articles which speaks about the old bridge, the assassination of Hema ,consequences and the objects of the assassinated people, Abhi get distress with the articles which is fishy for Dhruv, then he went near to Abhi, Dhruv questioned Abhi that "everything alright?" she wept, Dhruv questioned that "what happened mam?" she took the article of Hemas's murder, Dhruv asked that " you know about the girl?" yes the girl who is my school friend and she is an IAS officer of Vellore district in 2003, we met in call, after our school days, she informed that "I had become an IAS officer, for that, I felicitated her then she invited me to her village, she told me with that I am going to my village for an issue, if you are interested accompany with me, I responded with "No" sorry, I can't because I have some duties or personal works and I am an psychologist so, I need to attend some patents, each day, and I hang back with the deal, after a month I read in a newspaper article, that the IAS officer of Vellore get assassinated in a mysterious manner, which is a storm for me, while the argument is going charlotte entered the room and firstly, she get anger with the moment, she hide the anger Dhruv questioned about the articles, she replied that it's all just for knowledge, then the doctor called with the name "Hema" then, she turn around and stared at Abhi, Yes, tell me Abhi, Dhruv gets offended with the moment, then Hema started to narrate the story. After the call, I had received another call, which was from my hometown, I get happy with the moment, who speaks like a candy, that we are prominent that our village girl gets into a superior post, which is a honour for our village, so we plan to make an event and we would like to invite you as chief guest for the event, I accept with the deal, then, I ensure with the date, then I had pass through my works, after some days, I traverl to my hometown with my mother, I enjoyed the nature, then I had a call that the reservoir get damage nearby town, could you please get over here, suddenly I travelled to the spot and verify with the damages, then I get verify with the quality of materials ,date of construction, any missing cases of persons, I get ensure with the information then passed to the higher officials, then I returned to the way to my hometown, then I pass over a bridge which looks weird manner of construction or type of old bridge, which I saw when I get off from my hometown in my childhood, which has no renovation till the moment, I get information about the bridge to my assistant, then we entered into the village, the people, youngsters who gave me a warm welcome, then I collected the issues of the village, some said me about the village condition, like no proper water, electricity facility, no proper common transportation, you may noticed that the bridge and road manner which is poor, I do notice with the issues, then they gave me the objection in written manner, then we had lunch together, then I enjoyed with the event, then they ask me to stay for a night in the hometown they arranged me a bungalow for the night, then I had a call from an unknown number in that I heard that" your deadline is soon," then I forwarded the contact with the cybercrime department, i asked to verify with the number, at night I heard some screaming voice, then I step down, then I noticed that my assistant gets assassinated in a mysterious manner, then with anxiety I searched for my mother, I get a torch and entered into my mother's room and get offended with the scene, she gets hang in the fan, then I found some bloodshed and a glass piece in the edge of the room, I contact with the police, unfortunately there no tower in the area, I get vanished from the place and I entered into my vehicle, where the chauffeur get murdered with a knife, then I drove the car to the out of the village, where, some people waiting to attack with the lamp fire, then I do reverse the vehicle, they throw the lamp fire over the car, then immediately I step out from the car, then I ran over the bridge, some hazardous weapon gets on my head and fall off, with pain I tried to escape from the place, then I noticed that some politicians, some hometown person who surround me, then they questioned like, being in a down category your attitude is tremendous, can't you be cooperate with the politics, some people said that because of this girl our category gets clumsy, in that a politician asked that would you like to cooperate with us or not? If not what's your death wish? "No", it's not a big deal, I need equality, a good politics, proper, qualified materials for government hospitals and roads. While the argument passed on the villagers and youngsters arrived near the bridge, then the masked persons and politicians vacate the place and I was unconsciously admitted to a nearby hospital, then after some moments my soul gets split from my body.

Dhruv gets distressed with the information, then Dhruv's father get entered charlotte's room Hema's emotion gets changed to anger to head!!!, Dhruv's father asked about the report of Charlotte, Abhi replied with it was perfect and had no issues, and he request everyone to appear for dinner, Dhruv questioned that "Hema, what happened why did you stare at him?" he replied nothing, shall we go, , while dining Dhruv questioned about the bridge and issues, he replied with the bridge was not built correctly and since the budget is not allocated, so it looks idol, not in usage. Dhruv questioned that who is Hema, suddenly, his emotion gets changed, hands gets shivered suddenly he step out from dinning, then Dhruv gets doubt on him, after dinning, all went for the bed, at night Dhruv, gets some screaming of his father, when he went to his father's chamber, his father gets vanished and he searched for Charlotte, there is no appearance of charlotte in her room, he found a paper clip with bloodshed, in the paperclip he noticed a line get highlighted "Ranganathan" which is the name of his father, who stab her with the knife and get arrested, who is in prison for 10 years, and get released because of political power, then Dhruv went into the nearby forest in search of his father he heard continuous screaming of his father, in a state he heard a melody song of unidentified voice, he follow over the voice which leads him to next to the bridge, where he saw the soul of Hema in vigorous manner, and he saw his father, who gets into pieces, Hema started narrating the story that he is the one who has steal the money which, I allocated for the village and his blood is poison like a snake, he acts like a genuine person in front of the people, after the event I get into his home to verify about the complaints and I questioned him that you are receiving the

allocation of money?. At first he refused, then I noticed a locker where we can store money and ornaments, then I fitted an audio jammer under the table, then I heard that, he invested and signed in the treaty with corporate sector, and buying some hazardous factories, which leads to cancer and radioactive waves, he found about the jammer, I ask about the money and the treaty, he refused my arguements,then he make a sketch for me, unfortunately I get into it. Now tell me whether my revenge is right, do you think that my project for development, is wrong? Alright, but where is the Central home minister? What he does do? He is hazardous

who gives fake reports of renovation of the bridge, the central minister who approves the fake reports and opens the old bridge with no renovation, now it's time to leave the world with satisfied emotion, thanks for your investigation and cooperation, after the soul gets satisfied, Dhruv elaborates about his father to his hometown people. And asked for sorry for his father's mistakes he changes the property to the name of the villagers, then he returned to the United States with charlotte and his mother.

THE END

CHAPTER TWO

THE JOURNEY OF LOVE (CHAPTER II)

Aadiv becomes the manager Of ADMS industries. While on other side in India, Aadiv's father makes arrangements for his marriage in a good family, almost every arrangement gets over and one fine day Aadiv's father dialled to him, says the information, Aadiv get to inform about his marriage before, because it is a sudden incident, and Aadiv gave a shock news, that he was married , h had a baby Gabriel, which was unbelievable news for his father and end up the call, his father Inform the news to her wife and both were getting drowned in tears , they think how to inform to the family. And Aadiv's mother had less impact, but his father get thinking of it continuously, one-day Aadiv's father went for a walk at that time he get a Heart failure and lies on the road, the neighbours took him to the hospital and they admitted him to the ICU causality unit , the doctor checks the patient and replies that its critical to survive, Aadiv's mother makes continuous calls, but Aadiv is carrying a meeting, after some time he saw the continuous calls from her mother, so he calls and questions that what happened? Why did you make continuous calls? Aadiv's mother in a sad and crying voice said that your father is in critical and may not survive long, so please arrive soon, Aadiv end up the call, and he returns home in an unhappy state, or crying state, he replies that my father is in the critical state, he may not survive for a long time, Lea give her hands and convince Aadiv, they went to reserve tickets, but due to rain and bad weather, the flight platforms are not available and they convey the information to his mother and his father is at death doorstep, he waited for his son, after 4 days with hurry!!, they get the boarding pass and they arrived to Chennai [India] after a day they arrived to the hospital slowly his eyes turn to Aadiv's face , he saw both Aadiv and his wife, holding Dhruv's hands and said that " stay long" and Aadiv with tears said that "I am sorry", to his father and his father withholding, Aadiv's hands get off. And while standing out, his mother says that his father told her that, I want to see Aadiv for last time, until my soul not get satisfies, Aadiv heart get into pieces , he went lonely and he screamed, he take over the event in grand manner,, after the traditional events after a month, he went to meet his friends, and they make Aadiv to enter into a wrong path, they told that to forget the worries make a fun time with us, that is to do be cheers with us, at first Aadiv get ignored, by convincing he get the alcohol and he drunk, he returns in an unconscious state Lea and Aadiv's mother get shocked, with the incident and they dropped him in the bed, after a day when he wakes up Aadiv's mother and his wife get offended with his activities so they make Aadiv as home arres and his mother, says please make do return to Europe which is safer for my son's life, for that Lea replied that Ok, but you and your younger son should accompany with us to Europe, At first, she ignored, but after some talks, she convinced and Aadiv's younger brother doing catering and he owned a small restaurant, one day lea and Aadiv's mother talks about the issue to his Younger son, he gets accepted. He requests his childhood friend to supervise the restaurant, and Lea applied for passport and Visa, after all progress they give release from home arrest, under both Lea and Aadiv mother's home and they arrive to France and Aadiv's mother gets a warm welcome by Lea's family and they gave a feast to all, they took some rest for days, after some days lea shows Aadiv's mom and brother the whole city and both gets delight and enjoyed the monuments, after they travel through RER, the fastest express and they take dinner in the hotel, they return home at night ,the next day Lea and Aadiv get the blessings from Aadiv's mother and they started managing their works, on the other day, Lea took Aadiv's mother, to her company and he shows that how company get works and she gives blissful surprise to Aadiv's mother that his state in the company, his mother gets happy, to see him in such state and she feels him like a king and she thanked lea for showing such scenario, they return home, but his mother feel her husband is not available to see such scenario. After some days his younger brother plans to start a restaurant, he asks Lea about the issue , terms and conditions to start a hotel, she helps to Aadiv's brother, that time Lea's father get ignored with Aadiv's brother's decision and gets anger with lea, that time lea said about Aadiv's brother, that he studied for catering and he owned a restaurant which is running successfully in India and her father gets amazed,he Felicitated for his job and Aadiv's brother thanked lea for her help, they prefer plot which has the place of people gathering spot so,they choose beachside to construct a restaurant and they plan to construct and architect in an unique manner ,they start the work of construction, and work is going on and other side the industries gets more demand and profits so, they organized for an Party at the hotel that time Pub facility too arranged for the moment, Aadiv get self-control and place is surrounded by Lea's family so, he maintain silence and when they return home lea said that she feels happy that, he had not intake the glass of alcohol and Aadiv make silence ,makes a smile and they went to the home and after some days, on the day of restaurant inauguration, Lea's family and Aadiv with his mother get arrived to the inauguration and they arranged for party and it is an basic culture of France, Aadiv get excited and get overdrunk and he make a dance which became an abnormal to Aadiv's mother and lea drag him separately and gave slapping and locked him in the restroom and she went after the function gets end Lea and Aadiv's mother came to restroom and unlock the door and she sprinkles water and told to do promise that he wouldn't consume any alcohol and they left the place the next day, he woke up and the house is filled with silence, all stares at Aadiv and when he near to talk the person get vanished and his mother in top of anger and not yet talk for some days and he realizes his mistake and he asks sorry for his misbehaviour and his job get smooth and the ratio of products gets increases and whilw he returning to home, he met his school junior and he talks with him for some time and he gets the contact with Aadiv, and the next day its Aadiv's mother's birthday and he surprises with an unexpectable present and he organizes a party and they get celebrated well, and after some days Lea returns to home after finishing her job she gets kidnapped by a gang after few hours Lea's father had a call that "we had kidnapped your daughter", we need 1.5 billion euros within 2 days, if you didn't do then forget about your daughter, we tell you the place in the next call", and they end up the call. And Lea's father get nervous and he pass the info, to Aadiv and lea's father requests that get with police and Aadiv said first to be seated and he give some water and he replied please make confidential and don't be panic and while in the conversation, the telephone get rings and they records the conversation and the kidnapper that" don't be smart and don't track us" and get to downstairs and you will get a courier and get check with it, and the kidnapper gets off and they get a courier in that, there is a bag, a stethoscope and they had code word 9E20S66 and they get a call from kidnapper " take the money to avenue victor Hugo, Bordeaux and you should meet a person with red hat and White coat who is seated in a car and the number plate is AB-344-CA" and Aadiv inform to a special squad and he went to Bordeaux and he met a person with red hat and white coat and he asks the code and he says 9E20S66 and they went to a place filled with silence and they entered into an apartment and they walk in the stairs and they reached 17th floor and they check Aadiv and they enter him, the kidnappers are with black masks they said that to drop the bag and to move backward suddenly he drops and he grasps the gun from one kidnapper and he secure lea and he gets shot in his right arm and after 10 minutes he get protected lea and he gave the indication to the the squad and they appreciate Aadiv for his job, and he get a reward from European government andhis mother, lea and her family gets proud and the life turns smooth.

THE END

By:

Jeevanandham. G

9 798889 757030

Printed by Libri Plureos GmbH in Hamburg,
Germany